No veil ﹀

James L Duffy

I perch upon some drier shore,

watching as I drown.

Another me plunges deep,

pulling this me down.

Introduction

I have stared at a blank page for days now wondering how to introduce this story. Because that is what it is. A story. There is both fiction and truth in it. I hope this story needs no explanation. I do not expect everyone to understand it. I do not expect the story itself to make sense. It is a dark reality mixed with stark fantasy. I hope it will make sense to the people I am writing it for.

This story has been described as a 'thrilling, absorbing, and attractive novelette' which is 'fascinatingly isolating' and 'provokes introspection' by professionals. This is my first attempt at anything like this and as such I have utilised the tools at my disposal to make this product as widely available as I can.

The only thing I would say is that a large section of the story is structured in two columns down the page. I ask that you read this as a two contrasting voices in a dialogue with each other, and not as two separate columns. The pages will be structured in such a way to help with this understanding of the story.

To you, the reader, I ask that from here on out you picture me as a faceless shadow holding a pen and telling you a story. In these pages I am not one person, but many. I hope you read it.

*

.

<u>Prologue</u>

When I was younger (younger than I am now anyway) I used to create games in my imagination to entertain myself. I used to tell myself stories and build entire fictional universes in my mind and plot out entire franchises. This did not happen overnight. This was spanned out over almost a decade. I used to create fictional characters and give each one a character and a personality unique to them. These imaginary people were the closest friends I ever had.

I chose this path. I preferred this path. Over the years I drifted in and out of many real friend groups and every one of them gave me something, in their own way. However, just as easy as drifting into these groups I would also drift away just as easily. I was a perpetually lonesome introverted person, especially from a young age. I preferred imagination to reality. This is where our story begins.

With my own company to keep I would create ways to entertain myself, and there was a game I played once. My mind is foggy with the details of where and when this game came from. I do not remember the name of this game. I do not remember where I learned the rules. It may have been a game I created myself. I just do not remember.

For this game to work I had to choose a long stretch of road, more than one mile long. I then marked two x's in chalk on either side of this mile road. I distinctly remember making the decision to use dark red chalk. This was all done in the afternoon of a clear dry day so the rain would not wash away the chalk. I also made sure to choose a relatively straight road with little bends or curves.

At exactly one o'clock in the morning I stood at one x and whispered a phrase three times to the darkness around me. The phrase was 'Let my trial begin'. Each time I paused, only slightly to let it linger in the air. 'Let my trial begin'. Silence from all corners of the night. 'Let my trial begin'. I started to walk.

The goal of this game was to walk from one x, slowly and calmly, to the other without straying from the path. It sounds simple enough. At this time in the morning the roads and pavements would be deserted. I instinctively chose a stretch of road which had little traffic during the day, so it would be a rare occurrence to see anybody at night.

The first few minutes walking were easy enough. My body was numb with the cold. I would just try to keep moving at a steady pace, never looking back.

At the halfway point the hairs on my neck started to prickle. I began to hear things that were not there. I could see things moving in the distance. I could feel someone breathing on my neck. Each step was getting heavier as I continued. My heart began to race and beat against my sweaty t-shirt. I could not run. If I ran, I instantly failed. Shadows began to creep from the darkness towards me. The darkness closed in around me. Streetlamps flickered and died. My goal remained clear in my mind. However, as my imagination spiralled, creatures began to form from the horizon. They would bleed out from the gutters below me. Large monstrous mounds of crimson tar oozing from the edges of my darkness that would solidify and lurk just outside of my peripheral vision. The stars in the sky became a thousand blinking eyes watching me from above. The clouds became large skeletal claws scratching for my soul. The straight stretch of road began to twist and turn ahead of me. Pavement became quicksand. The trees at the clearing were smirking vicious grins.

I could see the second x only a few feet away from me.

If I had made it to the second x, then everything would be fine. They would all disappear. The monsters of my psyche would be dragged back to the darkness they came from. I would have faced my demons and won. The lowest corners of my sanity would have been emptied out and I would have made it through.

I played this game only once. I never did make it to that second x.

*

Part 1

The sky ignites in a sea of crimson ash.

Everything solid crumbles and fades around me, into darkness. I am completely alone here.

The pavement under my naked feet sparks and burns away, leaving only charcoal embers. This wasteland of destruction and chaos spans for miles in every direction. My skin starts to boil and flake revealing harsh slimy scales. In the distance there is a figure dragging a lifeless body along behind it. I prowl towards them. The figure is frantic and shapeless. It has a form consisting of only dust and smoke. As I rally myself ready to pounce on my prey, I notice two things:

The shadow figure has a face. Clear as day. It is frozen in horror by some half-forgotten scream. It is a face I knew. It is a face I once remembered.

The lifeless body it drags along behind it is me. A younger me, with shoulder-length hair and smooth teenage skin. The wrinkles of time have yet to leave its scars upon this me. The eyes, although closed, are not heavy and laden with woe. It is a peaceful harmless me.

The truth dawns on me. I am no longer me, and neither is he. The shadow turns away and continues on as if I am not there. It does not see me. I am unsure if it has the ability to see. Am I here? This place seems false and true all at the same time. The edges of the horizon blur and merge together. The dark and light mix together as one. I pounce.

Sinking long black claws into the beautiful innocent neck of the younger, unconscious, me, I rip and tear at the flesh. He chokes on a gurgling scream as dark crimson blood oozes from his mouth. The blood trickles down his cold lifeless chin and drips onto the ash with a faint hiss.

Laughing, I slowly peel its face off with my skeletal claws and place it delicately onto my own. A mask. A lie.

The shadow figure has stopped walking and stands motionless. Instead of a face frozen in scream the figure now looks burdened with sorrow. Teardrops of smoke appear from its eyes. As its tears fall, the shadow of me disappears into nothing.

I am finally alone now. Completely alone. Crouched upon the corpse of faceless younger me I howl into the abyss. His body starts to deteriorate rapidly. The flesh melts into bones and then those bones begin to snap and break with the weight of it all. The mask I am wearing stings my eyes. It hides my own crimson tears. I now know what I truly am. I am doomed. I am no longer human. I am no longer me.

Somewhere in this terrifying wasteland a single black raven watches on, as my sobs sharpen and crack into some maddened cackle. Fully transformed, I dance gleefully on top a mountain of bones. A sea of dead me.

*

Rainwater drains down the gutter between two nightclubs. A crowd of spectators have gathered on the surrounding pavement. Like some unseen prey, they remain frozen out of sight. Most of them just watch. Some try to video the unfolding scene in front of them.

"Can you feel it?

Three heavy-set men circle what appears to be a pile of damp bloodied rags dumped on the cobblestones. The ragged creature convulses with broken laughter. It pulls itself up onto its feet, spitting out some teeth, and shakily beckons its attackers forward.

You're completely alone. There isn't anybody wants to help you anymore. You hear me? You're on your own pal. Hell, you've been on your own a while now. Your whole life even.

The first, and largest, charges forward and slams the creature into a parked car. With a muffled crunch, the attacker stumbles over the creature. It turns, ready to attack. His two friends are moving lightly on the spot. They seem to be dodging and weaving back and forth; waiting for an opportunity to join the fight.

The crowd has doubled in size. Drawn out to the commotion and chaos they gather together like some sort of herd.

The largest attacker is hammering his fists against the creature's unconscious face, letting out a wounded roar as it does.

Chaos ensues.

Not even one hour ago, the street was deserted and silent. It is a Sunday night. The only noise was coming from the bar on the corner. A family gathering. A wake. The family had all gathered together to mourn. The largest of them, the father, was the quietest. He blames himself for what happened. It gnaws away at his conscience.

The mother has stopped socializing all together. She locked herself inside her own mind and refuses to eat.

The two brothers are confused. They want answers. They want someone to blame.

However, this night of silent mourning was interrupted by a drunken idiot. An old school friend of the deceased, who staggered into the wake unannounced, and uninvited. This idiot has started an argument with the father which eventually erupted onto the street outside. The father and his two sons then proceeded to teach this drunken idiot a lesson.

.

Even your pals have up and left you. Hell, one of them away and took the side-door out of this place you call life.

He chose a leap of faith over sticking by your side. You killed him. You know that? He was crying out for help. He was crying

out for someone to listen, and you ignored
it. You ignored him. You let it happen.

Assisted murder they call that.

Get up! You deserve every single bruise
you get. Pull what's left of you up and
face the music. Get back into the ring.
The bell has not rung.

They walking-steroids on legs haven't
finished beating seven shades out of you
yet. There is still candy left in this
piñata. You're going to spill it all. You're
going to spill it for them.

What's one more punch? One more hit.
You can take it. You're numb to it all now
anyway.

What is it you said to them again?

Something about him being a coward. You
told them he took the cowards way out.

Sorry pal, but you were kind of asking for a beating there. You got what you deserved.

Six years you were pals with him in school and he chose to hurt you. He chose to hurt all of you. You knew it was happening. You saw it with your own two eyes, and you did nothing. You let it happen. You could have stopped it. You could have said something.

Anything.

You were too busy in your own boring excuse of a life to even ask if he was okay. You were selfish. You didn't care about him. You don't care about him now either.

Pull yourself up and accept who you are. Accept what you are. You are a punching bag! An old worn-out battered punching-bag. Accept every punch thrown. Accept it with a bloody smile.

You never had a lot going for you, but boy can you take a punch. You excel at being someone else's punching bag. You can take an inhumane amount of pain and not even flinch. Nobody can knock you down. Not when you are already at rock bottom. Drag yourself back up and dust yourself off. This party is far from over.

The crowd has long since dispersed into the chilly night air. Two of the Bouncers working doors have come out and cornered the three men. The father is being pinned down by one, while the other two are talking to the second bouncer.

Two police cars and an ambulance pull up on the corner. The officers split up. One talks with the bouncers while the other closes off access to the area.

Pull yourself up and keep on smiling.

In the distance, unnoticed by anyone, the creature has found his feet and has staggered down the alley towards the other end. Not a creature, but in fact a young man; he turns and glances back towards the scene before cautiously heading into the night.

Because the world is going to keep on punching."

*

*

About an hour has passed.

The young man seems to have regained partial control of his body. The slow agonising walk home has sobered him up. Still bruised and bleeding, he favours his left leg more.

"That tingling feeling in your arms and legs is not pins and needles. It is the alcohol wearing off. You're sober now.

The walk home was uneventful. Nobody seemed to be chasing him. No sirens in the distance. Nobody in the family knew who he was so he was fine.

All they punches will have tenderised you. A prime piece of meat. A rare mutton-chop. Pummelled to perfection. You suit pain. You wear it well. It's always been easier to wear than your own skin. You slip easily into it, like you've wore it for years.

He reaches his parents' house. His house. There is a light on in the living room. The curtains are drawn but there are definitely raised voices. It must be well past midnight.

Lights are on. That can only mean one thing, and you know it. They're up. Probably waiting on you to come back so they can start round two.

Taking a steadying breath, he tries to compose himself as best he can. He tries to wipe away the crusted blood as best he can.

You're definitely not ready for this minefield that awaits. You're still going to try and pass unnoticed, aren't you?

He opens the front door.

The door catches on something and will not open fully. He uses his weight to push it the rest of the way. Stumbling over something on the carpet he regains his feet and takes in the full scene unfolding around him.

A shirtless reflection of him is seething with rage as it stands over an unconscious body. The body is lying at an odd angle. It looks like it has been dragged into the hall.

"I've killed 'm" is all the shirtless reflection can mutter.

In the living room another reflection is flapping its arms like a bat and screeching insults. Behind this reflection, in a chair, is an elderly reflection shivering under a blanket. The older reflection is openly crying. The carpet is damp and stained with an upturned wine glass. There are definitely words being shouted by the flapping reflection, but nothing sounds familiar. Nothing makes sense.

All of his reflections are panicking and restless. His shirtless reflection has slumped against a wall and is sitting with his head in his hands.

It was easier back out there. Would you no rather go another round with steroid and sons than deal with this?

After the shortest of pauses to take in everything, the young man steps over his unconscious reflection and heads into the kitchen. He picks up a dusty glass from the sink and fills it with water. Catching his real reflection in the mirror he watches his expression steel over and harden. His face looks older than his years. Tired eyes and the beginning of frown lines. He drinks the water in one gulp and then heads back out into the hall.

You don't see them, do you? They're not really there are they? The lot of them. Come on, let's deal with this.

He crouches down beside his unconscious reflection and lifts him up. Instinctively his shirtless reflection lifts the other end. They carry the body into the living room and place him onto the couch. Checking for a pulse, he is satisfied the reflection is not dead.

The flapping reflection has swooped down onto the couch and is pushing them both away. It is screeching into his shirtless reflections face. He stands up and turns towards his elderly reflection, who is still openly sobbing. He checks to make sure they are okay. The flapping reflection is still screeching insults and death threats as they try to coo over the unconscious reflection.

The young leaves the sitting room and stops in the kitchen to lean against the counter. His shirtless reflection has disappeared. He possibly thought best to go to bed. His unconscious reflection will be okay. This is nothing that hasn't happened before. His flapping reflection will be insufferable for days now.

Opening the fridge, he picks up a pack of cheap energy drinks and heads back towards the sitting room. It has quietened down as there is soft soothing noises coming from the flapping reflection. He passes by and crouches down beside his elderly reflection. It seems to be sleeping. He tries his best to clean the spilled drink around them. He nods to himself more than anybody else, standing up and turning only to be confronted by his flapping reflection.

"HOW DARE YOU!!" it wasn't a question.

He pushes them out of the way like they aren't even there and makes his way upstairs.

His shirtless reflection is loudly snoring from the back room as he listens at the door. Content in the knowledge this should be the end of it tonight he enters his own bedroom and shuts the door with a click.

Collapsing onto a couch in the back of the room where a bed should be, he lets out a deep sigh. His real reflection in the full-length mirror on the cupboard door stares back at him for a few moments. His shirt is caked in a cocktail of sweat and blood.

Opening a can of energy juice, he winces as he pulls his coat off. He is tired. He is sore. He want's nothing more than to sleep.

It's quiet. Too quiet.

Delicately he pulls himself back up and opens the bedroom door. He pulls a chair over to face the hall and reluctantly sits down. Sounds of muttered voices can be heard from the living room.

He listens. He waits. It's going to be a long night.

You know this is only the beginning. They are going to wake up. They are going to be angry. They are going to want round two. You are sound asleep in the next room there. You could scream and shout bloody murder. You are out cold. You won't be able to wake. You wouldn't see it coming. Nobody would. You're the only one able to stop it if it happened.

Are you just going to sit here and see what happens? See how it plays out?

What if your reflection climbs those stairs? What if he comes up here demanding another match? You are going to be the only thing between him and disaster. Whatever the fight was about originally you don't remember, but you are happy to let it continue? Are you a coward? Frozen to this chair, too scared to move? Too scared to act.

Nah. You'll do it alright. You'll step between the two of them. You'll kill him if that's what it takes. He is just meat and bones. One good punch and you would finish him. You could destroy him. CRACK! You would snap him in two. But you're not thinking about that. No. You're thinking about the banister at the top of the stairs. Nice shiny banister.

One good push and he would fall.

You could push him over before he even knows what's happened.

You would watch in slow motion as he fell to his death. Fear in his eyes as the lock with your own.

His bones would crumble as he hit the stairs on the way down. Your other reflections would come hurtling out the corners of this house. They would wake the dead with their screams. Still, that's not a good enough end for him though. You would watch the light leave his eyes. You would pretend you were shocked. You would pretend you cared. However, you would just be cold and numb. You wouldn't be happy. You wouldn't be sad. You would just be numb.

They would call the police on you.

They would arrest you. They would probably piece together that you were involved in the incident earlier tonight. You would get charged and they would stick you in jail. You would rot there alone.

Still nothing?

Energy drinks won't help you. You've not slept well in months. Caffeine just fuels the hatred inside of you.

Let's face it. You're not going to do a thing. They're sleeping down there. If not, they will be too far gone to remember everything that happened tonight. You've just wasted your night, waiting on nothing. It will all be forgotten by lunchtime. They'll have forgotten it all. Same thing happens every week. You're going to have to watch them forget it happen and then a repeat performance next week all over again.

It never happened.

You won't forget it though. You will be stuck here in this moment. You will be left to stew in foolish anger.

You going to kill him? What then? You going to run? You've nowhere to go. Sorry to admit it but nobody wants you. This is the only doorstep you can darken with your shadow. It's the only place that will take you. You know it's true. You're one of them. Even though you fight hard to deny it you are here for life.

You'll forget about it eventually. Just like you're supposed to. Just like they all do.

Seconds have bled into hours as early morning sunlight creeps in through the blinds. Checking his watch, the young man bins the last empty can of energy juice and picks up his rucksack.

Glancing into the living room he checks on his reflections, quietly sleeping, and then heads out into the morning.

*

You've got nobody but me. I am not going anywhere.

*

The walk to college was both brisk and numb. He was lost in some faraway daydream imagining some fantastical adventure. Another life. Another time. The road to college was a familiar one, and he did not have to concentrate on where he was going. He could have closed his eyes and trusted muscle memory to know the way. Along the main road and past the library. Past the court and through the dam. Past the station and straight onto the main college campus. It was a blur of colour and noise he had become accustomed to.

Arriving outside the classroom he realised he was about an hour early. After a few moments he settled himself down on the cold stone corridor floor beside the door and closed his eyes.

There's no escaping it. Even imaginary escaping... they'll find you.

You would be out of place anywhere else. You know these roads like the back of your hands. You could walk them blindfolded. It just shows how pathetic this existence really is. If all you ever do is walk from house to college and back again.... there's nothing in between.

Mr Grey, who was a grizzled veteran of college tutoring and had worked for some of the biggest television stations in the country, made his usual morning patrol through campus. From the outside he looked like a regimented man with very little patience for laziness. He did not like what he could not fully understand or explain. It was only this year and this new semester when his path crossed with a curious young man.

He was indeed a bright young man but utilised his talents in the wrong way. He had a flair for illusions and sleight of hand. If only he would focus on coursework, he would be top of the class.

It always took exactly nineteen minutes and twenty-six seconds to make his way from his car to the classroom door. He was always the first one there to set up, in advance for his students arriving. It was, however, rather odd to notice the young man sitting by the classroom door this early before class. Nodding, as the young man glanced up, Mr Grey opened the classroom door and went in. He shut it sharply behind him.

They say college is meant to open doors. Not close them in your face.

The young man sat for a few moments, wondering if he should follow or not. A few seconds passed in his mind, but the clock had moved at least half an hour. The other students began to arrive. She was there too. The only girl in his class. She was nothing perfect, but she had stolen part of his attention from the moment they first met. She was a few years older and was the quiet nerdy type. In the three months he had been studying at the college he had spoken a total of fourteen words to her. The group of boys she was with stopped in front of the door, and she smiled down at him. He knew she always liked his illusions.

Don't even think about it pal. She's way out your league anyway. What do you even know about her? You've spoken more to your postman than you have to her. We both know you're only sticking this course out because of her. You hate this course. You're failing, and she is definitely not falling.

The classroom door opened, and Mr Grey looked around at everyone for a few moments before stepping aside to let them into the classroom. The young man pulled himself to his feet and declared:

"Sir, I have another magic trick!" He smiled shyly as he stared at the shoulder of the girl in front of him.

Mr Grey studied his expression for a second or two before folding his arms and sighing defensively.

"If you must. Get on with it."

I bet you have those cards on you. Don't you? Never missing an opportunity to be the class clown. You're nothing more than a dancing pony.

He now had the attention of the whole class. They were all standing around him as he fished a packet of playing cards from his bag. He took them out and fanned them in front of Mr Grey.

"A normal deck of cards."

"Doubtful but continue."

"If you inspect these cards I assure you, you will find nothing wrong. Fifty-two cards. They are all there and well mixed. Sir, pick a card and show it to the others please. Don't say the card aloud. Keep it to yourselves."

Mr Grey leaned forward and chose a card at random. He glanced down at the card and then towards the young man.

"Can you show the card to the class. I won't look."

He turned away and faced the vending machines opposite the classroom door. Mr Grey showed the card to the rest of the class. Three of Spades. He turned back around and held out the pack of cards. Mr Grey instinctively put the card back into the pack. He shuffled the cards without paying attention.

Dance pony! Dance!

"Lady…, and gentlemen. Boys…, and girl. I have no way of knowing what card Mr Grey chose. But with a little magic we can transport this card from this pack and send it somewhere new. I need someone with magic inside of them."

You're really putting in the overtime to get a moment of her attention here are you not? She doesn't care.

His eyes locked with hers and he smiled.

"Can you take the pack and tap it three times."

Gently, she took the pack and tapped the top three times.

"Can you now look through the deck for the card. Do not tell me what the card was. Just try and find it in the deck."

The class watched as she rifled through the pack for the three of spades without finding it.

You getting ready for the big reveal?

"From the silence I assume the card is not there. Would you be amazed if I could transport the card into Mr Greys pocket? That would be too easy. What if it was in one of your backpacks? Still too easy. Hmmm, magic really can be thirsty work."

The class watched as he walked up to the vending machine and tapped the glass. He tried to open it, but it wouldn't budge. He turned back to the class.

"Anyone want a drink?"

A hand shot up and someone says the name of a drink. Without missing a beat, he turned and put money into the machine choosing the drink chosen. He pulled the drink out and turned back to the class. He opened the bottle and took a long slow drink, revealing the card inside of the bottle.

Thank you, Dave. You're the only one foolish enough to play along with this crap.

Fidgeting for a moment with the bottle so that the damp card comes out, he reveals it to be the three of spades.

Silence. The class erupted in applause as he binned the bottle.

Mr Grey nodded his approval and tried to regain his composure. The young man took the deck of cards back and pocketed them.

A tiny bit of confidence can be dangerous. Don't do it.

"I was wondering…"

His hand began to shake as he tried to look at her.

"I was wondering if you wanted to go for lunch sometime?"

A pained expression. The girl apologised. She explained she was dating someone. She did not look at him as she spoke. He nodded. They were the last two in the corridor. She turned into the classroom and left him there alone.

Mr Grey came out to investigate.

Told you! Now do what you do best and run. Run away!

"Sir, I wanted to say to you at the end of class but thought it would be best to tell you now. I got the confirmation about that full-time apprentice opportunity. It's something I don't want to miss out on. I'm sorry but I think I have to drop out of college. I hope you understand."

Mr Grey nodded. He knew the young man had become lost in the class weeks ago. It was a shame. However, if the young man was able to pursue another dream, then he could not stop him.

"You're a bright student. If you ever need someone to talk to, my door is always open."

They shook hands. He turned away and started walking.

*

He was just patronizing you there. If you need someone to talk to? No problem mate! You'll be top of the list. The unemployment office has started asking for references now. Idiot.

So, what exactly is your plan now then?

You are up diarrhoea creak without a boat, let alone a paddle. You just burnt the last of your bridges there. Good luck explaining this to your family. You'll have to start looking for a job first thing Monday. What was that crap about apprenticeships? A lot of lies you made up on the spot to look like you've got a plan. You've no education! You've no friends! You've no love life! As I said before it's just you and me pal. You better get used to it.

*

This walk home seemed different. It seemed longer. He dragged his feet heavily as he walked. The house was deserted this time. He checked about to see if he could find any trace of what happened the previous night. Nothing. Nothing. They would be at work. He would have been hungover and have one beast of a headache, but he would still have made it to work. His other reflections would have retreated to quieter pastures and be waiting for the storm to pass. They may have made a detour to the local hospital for a check-up, but that was too much like common sense.

You messed up! Good and proper! Now man up and deal with it.

Nobody. Nobody is home. They did clean up after themselves though.

They will not be back for a while. You may have chased them off for a while now.

After checking each room individually in case any reflection was hiding, he checked the fridge and then slouched on the sofa facing the television. He spent a few minutes silently flicking through channels until the front door burst open. A reflection swooped in and discarded their coat on the couch before disappearing back out into the hallway. He strained to listen for a few moments, turning the television back off and taking a long breath, as he knew what was about to come next.

Empty. You've got the house to yourself, and you choose to shut the world out and stuff your fat-ass with snacks.

Glass in hand and a smirk on its face the reflection closed the door behind itself as it entered the sitting room, shutting off his exit plan.

Good luck. You're not going to be able to ignore this forever.

"SO…?" It was not a question.

He turned towards his reflection and raised an eyebrow. Silently gesturing 'what' as it watched him. This just made it angrier.

"SO…, are you not going to apologise?" it spat.

"Apologise for what exactly? What? What do you want me to apologise for? For dealing with this cluster-fuck of a situation I walked into last night. For making sure you didn't kill someone. For stopping you killing yourself. For helping. What exactly do I need to apologise for? You're drunk… again… and just want someone to fight. Actually, you don't want a fight. You just want me to sit there and take it. You want somebody to fight… at. You want a pin cushion to verbally abuse and expect me to take it."

His reflection let out a shriek and slapped him once across the face with the palm of its hand. It was an odd sensation being slapped by yourself. The young man just stood up and walked past it. He could easily move it out of the way and open the door. He let out a deep sigh as he accepted another night in his room, resigned to watching old DVDs alone.

To be fair, you should apologise. You're glued to a sinking ship. The cracks are showing and it's going down.

Don't know why you're wasting your breath here pal. He is not listening. He'll not hear a word you say. You would be better talking to a brick wall. You might even get a stimulating conversation from the wall.

And just like that… you run. Turn tail and run.

"You caused that fight last night! You! We were having a good night and then it all went sour. Because of you."

"Did I miss the memo? Am I a few chapters behind everybody else? If you want to know what happened to me last night, then I'll tell you. I got my arse royally handed to me last night outside of some bar. I got drunk and started a fight that I then epically lost. I then limped all the way home to this circus when I had to deal with more crap! I dealt with it. Not you. Not them. Me. Nobody else was capable of helping so I did it. You want to live life like it's a constant party, and when the shit hits the fan, you blame everyone but yourself. You are all a joke! You are only here to make my life a misery. Every day I wake and you're there. I can hear you at night fighting with one another as clear as day! I never realised it until I was older, but I now see it for what it is. Anybody and everybody with an ounce of common sense ran for the hills when they realised how toxic this poison really is. If I had an ounce of self-respect, I would run for the hills at the first opportunity. I no longer see the truth for what it is. I see you as a liability. I spend my nights waiting for the next fight. I wait for the next war. So, tell me… what do I have to apologise for?

You didn't do anybody any favours. They would have dealt with it, or forgot it ever happened. He's just pissed that you will remember it. You'll remember it and use it as ammo in future fights. He hates knowing you're right. He hates that you can win an argument every single time.

Just apologise and we can move on. He will forget this by the time the others get home.

His reflection, who was glaring viciously at him throughout, wobbled on the spot for a moment. Its eyes lost focus and glazed over. Something was wrong. Something was seriously wrong. It seemed to forget he was there. Looking through him, it tried to step towards him. Its movements became animated. It was almost ghostly. A hand moved towards his lips as it made a dabbing motion with its fingers to the side of his mouth.

I think you've knocked him silly. He deserved it.

He stood, frozen to the spot, as he watched in horror. He repeatedly mouthed his own name as things got progressively worse.

Their eyes locked. The reflection regained some grasp of reality as a slow trickle of blood crept out the corner of its mouth. It opened its mouth as if to speak. Blood. Black. Dark. Thick. It came oozing out of its open lips, like crimson tar.

Ah shit. You've no knocked him silly I think you've away and killed the dick.

Time froze. The young man made to dive towards his reflection to stop it falling. The reflection folded at the knees.

"Help. Help. HELP. HELP. HELP. HE-ELP!!!"

His reflections chin was caked in thick dark blood as its eyes lost focus again and rolled backwards into its head. He cradled its lifeless body. He screamed. He punched the floor. He shook the reflection to try and wake it. He dragged it into the centre of the room, screaming its name as he did. His reflection did not hear him.

A passing neighbour heard the commotion. The neighbour ran towards the commotion and into the house. A moment of silence passed as the neighbour stopped to take in the scene. He was covered in blood. He was desperately trying to wake his reflection.

"What happened?

"I killed it. I think I've killed it." Is all he could say through the tears.

Other neighbours had arrived at the sound of the young man's screams. The first neighbour immediately dialled for an ambulance as two others tried to pull him away from his reflection. They eventually succeeded. He made towards the front door to vomit. The neighbours then called some other people. He slid down the outside wall and slumped on the top floor of the steps. He sat in his vomit, not even noticing. After some time, another reflection rushed past him into the house.

Screaming isn't going to bring him back. You caused this. You killed him. He's going to die in your arms, and you don't have a clue what to do. You will never forgive yourself for this.

Two paramedics arrived. His brother arrived and lit a cigarette by the gate. The neighbours left one by one. The two medics carried the reflection out on a stretcher. Another reflection followed and said something as it passed. He was not listening. His brother said something, and he just nodded. They left. They all left. He was left alone on the front steps numb to the world around him.

Everything you touch breaks, doesn't it? It turns to ash in your hands. Just don't dare touch me with those hands. He was due one of these turns soon anyway. You're just the unlucky sod that had to deal with it. You panicked. Like a scared child you panicked. If it wasn't for your squealing, He'd be dead. I mean really dead. I suppose it is a good thing. You saved his life. You almost killed him, but you saved his life by squealing like that. He'll never thank you, by the way. Nobody will thank you. When he gets out, they'll all pretend like it never happened. Your brother might be the only one who will mention it. Even though he's away living his own life. In those rare moments he will try and tell you that you're not a complete waste of space. You know differently though. You know you caused them to collapse. He's been on the ledge for a while. You just pushed him over it.

By fighting him you slowly kill him. You are the final nail in his coffin.

A few days ago, you even asked yourself if you would ever hug him again. If you would ever be able to accept him again.

A few hours had passed. His brother arrived back and sat beside him on the front steps.

"It's going to be okay. Nothing they've not seen before. It's going to be okay. Thanks to you. If you had not shouted for help…," He lit a cigarette "He's going to stay a bit longer. Talk to the doctors for a bit. I said I would come back and check on you. We all left in a rush, and nobody really stopped to check you were okay."

He's a cockroach who will outlive what's left of you.

"…m fine."

A few moments of silence passed before his brother stood up and held out his hand.

"You need a drink. Come on."

*

That's what to do. Go down your sorrows with more alcohol. That worked so well last night. Go drink until you can't remember tonight. Go drink until you're another statistic.

*

It started to rain. He pulled a faded-grey hoodie tighter around him and zipped it up as he watched his brother light another cigarette.

"You'll get through this. We'll get through this,"

Nodding to himself, his brother turned and slowly stumbled down the road, heading home. It had been several hours of deep and heavy conversations, never truly touching the bottom. His brother told him he had just got a new job and would soon be moving out of town. It was only a few weeks away. They toasted new beginnings. He had lifted the glass to his lips but did not drink. They talked of college, and they joked about how he would graduate in no time and be free of this town. He still had not told anybody he had quit the course. His brother was proud of him. He did not want to ruin that.

So much for the only person you can openly talk to. You truly are alone now.

After a minute or so of watching his brother disappear into the darkness, he checked the time on his phone. It was late. The house would be empty and cold. The pool of crimson would still be there, staining the carpet beside the sofa. Broken glass shards would lay beside it, still crusted with skin and blood.

Smoke and mirrors. More lies. Sooner or later, you're going to have to come clean. Your life's a mess. You have nothing on every side of you. You're in an empty ocean and you're drowning. You cut off all your pals. You pushed them away. You're even pushing away the only person who you can talk to. Is it for your safety? Or his?

He pulled a slightly limp and damp cigarette from his pocket and placed it on his lips.

Lighting it, he admired the scene around him. It was a Monday night. The town was eerily quiet. A few stragglers here and there, moving quickly through the night chill. The bar he had just left was the same bar from last night. There was a large red and black poster on the wall outside. A man's face stared down at him. One side was calm and collected in black and white. The other was red and white with a face contorted and pained.

A shiver ran down his spine.

Turning away he decided he did not want to go home just yet. The darkness was quiet. Dead. There was nobody around to question him. Nobody about to notice the cracks. Pulling his hood over his head he shrugged against the cold and pushed onwards.

Faces faded in and out of his vision. He could hear the voices of distant memories. His arms were still sore as he shook his sleeves down even further and tried to ignore the chill on his neck. He kept to the shadows as he walked and only stopped when he noticed others in the distance.

The wet pavement squelched underfoot as he turned down an alleyway towards the local Dam. Someone's car alarm was shrieking in the distance. A young couple were walking towards him from the other direction. He had nowhere to hide this time. He kept his gaze at his feet. A duck was pecking away at an empty chocolate-bar wrapper. The young couple were laughing. It was some secret personal, joke. only they knew. They glanced over and noticed him.

Keep your eyes down. You don't want to ruin someone else's night.

He stepped to the left to let them past. He quickly glanced up to nod at them.

Ah crap.

Those eyes. He stopped. The couple stopped. A moment passed. The young man regained his composure. He smiled at them.

"Hey, it's been so long. How have you been?"

Her partner answered.

"You are?"

The girl was avoiding meeting both sets of eyes. He laughed.

"Hi… Sorry. It's been a bit of an odd day. I used to go to school with…. We used to hang out with the same group of friends."

Holding out his hand for her partner to shake, he waited. The partner looked at the hand and then back into his eyes.

"You're… him. Nah. You can't be him."

"I'm who, exactly?"

It became apparent that the partner had been drinking heavily that night. He was holding himself awkwardly. For a tall skinny young man, he was trying to puff himself out as much as possible.

Keep your mouth shut. Keep the head down. Keep walking. This is not going to end well.

If you ever did love her… if you ever felt anything for her… walk away. This idiot is drunk. He just wants to prove himself to her. Let him get it off his chest and move on. He'll forget about you tomorrow. This is not the same as last night. You can still walk away.

Time slowed down as several things happened all at once. The girl tried desperately to step between them. He dropped his hand to his side and shrugged it off. The partner had pushed himself forward to block the girl and was toe-to-toe with him.

"I heard stories. Stories about a creepy loner guy who used to hang about with her pals. Stories about a creepy guy who used to stare at my fiancé from afar. I never expected something as… pathetic… as this. So, why don't you away and crawl back to the hole you fell out of. She doesn't want you. She doesn't want to even know you. You caused her nothing but pain. She would never choose someone like you. I mean… look…"

Don't.

You're on your own from here on out. I am not having anything to do with what comes next. If you make it out alive, I'll see you later.

A high-pitched scream filled the air. He had knocked the partner to the ground. In some unexpected blind rage, he was repeatedly punching with every ounce of strength he had left. His fists smashed against the bloodied unconscious face. The girl tried to pull him off. There was nobody else around to help. The dam was deserted.

The girl collapsed in hysterical tears.

All she could do was try to slap him with all her strength in a poor attempt to stop him. His punches slowed down and he began to realise the damage he had done. The partner was no longer breathing. His face was covered in a mixture of blood, saliva, and tears. The girl was sobbing as she tried to push him off.

He stood up. The girl did not know what to do. All she could do was scream. She could try to call the police. Pounding at her partners chest she gulped against the burning stream running down her cheeks.

"G'outthway!" He had regained some of his composure.

She tried to fight him off, but he kept holding her back.

"STOP. HITTING. ME. I'M GOING TO SAVE HIS FUCKING LIFE!"

The girls' arms dropped to her sides as she watched in horror as he started CPR on her lifeless fiancé. Rain had started to beat down and wash the blood away. He was giving mouth-to-mouth as the car alarm in the distance went quiet.

Coughing up a cocktail of bloody rainwater her fiancé turned on his side to let the rest of the liquid pour from his mouth.

He stood. The girl crawled towards her fiancé, touching his shoulder as he vomited. Everything seemed to stop. Lying on the gravel beside them was her phone. Bending down he picked it up. He dialled emergency services. He stopped before pressing the call button. The girl he had secretly admired for over six years was still helping her fiancé. She had stolen his gaze from the first day of school and she never even knew it. However, reality beckoned.

He handed her the phone and nodded.

"Phone them. Tell them what happened. You know my name. You know who I am. Tell them what I did. Tell them everything. I'm sorry. I truly am. I never meant for any of this. Phone them. Please."

Taking her phone with a shaking hand she stared into his lifeless eyes. Something was now missing behind his eyes. He turned to walk away, glancing back as he did.

"Tell them they can find me at the train station. I promise I'll be there. I… I need to sort some things out first. If you ever had any feelings for me. If you ever cared, even a little, tell them where they can find me."

What have you done? You're definitely going to jail now. You couldn't just walk away.

Turning away from her the young man started running.

How does it feel knowing you destroy everything you touch?

*

*

The rain was getting heavier as the night went on. The young man was sitting on a bench at the local train station. He was bent over with his head in his hands, sobbing. Every now and again a lorry or car would speed past on the road behind him. The tracks would be flooded with the lights from the vehicles and then go dark again. They passed by unaware to his existence. Nobody knew he was there, except her. He had laid his belongings in a neat pile beside him on the bench. He covered them with his hoodie as he was now just wearing his soaked vest. His arms were covered with a collection of scars. Some of them had healed completely. Some looked fresher than the others. It was time.

Standing up he turned and watched as flashing blue and red lights approached from the distance. They could not have timed this better. He stood on the edge of the track and looked south towards the oncoming train. Its light seemed to focus his thoughts. He took a deep breath and closed his eyes.

You've really done it now. You've finally destroyed what was left of your pathetic excuse for a life. Nobody cares. Your family don't care. Your brother doesn't care. If you had friends, they wouldn't care either. But no... you cut them all off as soon they got close. You don't have a job. You have no future. Nobody loves you. Nobody to love. You don't care about yourself. Why the fuck should someone care about you?

You've burned your bridges. No more choices left. It's a lifetime sentence in a jail cell now for this. You'll crack in prison. You'll end up being a real punching bag in there. You can take a lot. I give you that. But you won't last a month in prison. You would snap. Looks like there's one road left. It's me and you. I'm here with you, whether you like it or not, until the end.

Think of all the good this one act will do. Your family will grieve for a day or two and then they can turn their lives around when they're no longer burdened with you. Your brother will be able to drop all ties to this town and start his new life.

Instead of being dragged down by having to babysit you all the time. The need of the many outweighs the need of the few as the saying goes. That's what your best at. You were put on this earth to be a punching bag. So, man up and take that final punch.

They say it's like falling asleep. You know that's a lie though. There will be pain. You'll feel it. It's the first thing you will feel in a long time. You were so shut off from everything and everyone that you ended up talking to me. The voice in the back of your head. That nagging whisper that most people ignore. You couldn't ignore me. I'm your only friend. I'm your final companion. You made damn sure of that.

Think of the girls who passed in and out of your life. The girls you would be fascinated with for months at a time. Why was it you were so fascinated with them? Did you think it was love? Did you think you loved them? You didn't even know them. They were shadows in the scenery around you, and nothing more. You wanted them to be a light. You hoped they noticed you.

You were jealous of them. They had something you never did. They were happy. They were normal. You were left with me in your head from the beginning and it has always been like this.

Think of how much good you'll be doing with this one moment. They will forget about you. You're another statistic. Think of their faces. All the faces of people you have known in this excuse of a life. They all blend into one, don't they? None of them meant anything to you. Think of that first moment you ever met each one. They can be happy again. They can all be happy again. You could be the reason why.

One step.

A leap of faith.

The light from the train floods the edge as he steps forward.

*

It'll hurt for a moment and then nothing. Darkness, everlasting, will consume you. The final sleep. Nobody can hurt you in there. Not even me. Nobody can hurt you when you're dead.

*

Part 2

Water. Scars crust over with the growing weeds as I drown. Earth. Charcoal sand drains from me as I gulp for … air. Sharks flap their wings in the sky above. Fire. The nightmare melts around me.

There is a mirror. I am afraid to look into it. I am surrounded on all sides by faceless lifeless mannequins. I have no shape or form. I just am. I try to look down at my body and hands but there is nothing there. Maybe it is a trick of my imagination, but the lifeless mannequins begin to move towards me.

Resigned. I look into the mirror. A young man looks back. I do not recognise him. He has a keen smile with bright eyes. His expression falters as he looks me up and down. His smile fades. His eyes dull over. Cracks begin to appear. His scars begin to show. He is ugly. A hideous creature with unusual features. Skeletal wings of oozing crimson tar protrude from his shoulders. His grin is crooked and vicious now. His eyes have tints of crimson in the pupil.

The image blurs and changes. A raven. One eye fixed on me. It lets out a startling call and takes flight.

The mirror is now a doorway. I step through it into another darkness. Nothing. I am still surrounded by faceless mannequins. Something has changed. Something is different. I quickly turn and look back at the doorway. Another me steps through the doorway towards me. He grabs me by the throat and lifts me off my feet. His face is contorted in a painful rage. I can feel the life draining from me as I try to say something. His grasp loosens. I drop through the floor, and I am falling.

I am falling. I can see people. Ghostly apparitions of other people falling beside me. They don't notice me. I notice them. I try to take in each of their faces as I speed past them. None of them are familiar. Strangers. We fall together.

I hit something solid. A tiled floor. My old school building. I am on my knees. The solid thing that hit me was my own fist. A younger me drags this me to my feet and slams me into the *wall. There is nothing human behind those eyes. Only darkness and rage. I catch my reflection in his pupils. I am not me. I am another student. A friend. A distant friend. Someone I pushed away. Someone who was lost. Someone who needed help. Someone I could not save.*

A raven swoops in and lifts me from my own grasp and bursts through the school ceiling and out into an ocean of drowning people. Each one of them is me. We fly over the looming darkness and onto an infinite highway. I watch as a younger me draws chalk outlines on a road and then begins to walk down it alone. He looks determined. He is being followed by something monstrous. There is nobody else here except the two of us.

The raven drops me.

As I fall through what I expect to be the last of my sanity, I expect no end to the drop. My body slams into the mud of some cemetery as the raven lands gently on top of a grave in front of me. The grave is empty, and so am I.

*

"I am born.

Like most things I am unsure of my beginning. I just am. Years of self-loathing and disgust birthed me into life. I am now forever attached to you. The first memory I have is that of a reflection in a mirror. Something behind his eyes birthed me into life. I do not know what.

He was too young to notice the world around him. He was too lost in his ignorance to care. He would hang around with the other local children. Some he knew from school. Some were through family friends. They would play silly childish games as I lurked in the corner. They would laugh and joke and he would remain none the wiser. Years went by and others would filter in and out of his orbit. Some would care about him. Some would not. He ignored most of them.

Around his second year in secondary school his path would cross with the first girl he ever really noticed. She would argue with him and then insult him for ignoring her. He was confused. He did not understand. I was drawn closer to him.

I followed. He would make a run of bad decisions. He chose to be a loner and even though he had friends in school he would never allow himself to be happy. He would rarely let anyone in. Even his closest friends were cut off when time came for it. However, it is here in the school grounds when we first officially met. He had been hiding feelings he had for a girl in his class for a year or so and never acted on it. Constantly conscious of his appearance and personality he chose to stop eating for days at a time. This is when the self-harming began. It was small at first. He would cut himself with the razor blade out of a sharpener as an experiment. He would punch brick walls. He would cut his feet. He would burn his skin in an attempt to feel something. Eventually he could hide this in plain sight with simple acts such as picking the skin on his feet and skin. He was losing part of himself, and his conscience was slowly becoming numb to the world around him. At this point in his life, I could almost place my hand upon his shoulder. Not quite yet.

One day he was walking through the school corridor and a friend playing a trick, tripped him up. For a moment our eyes met. For a moment we were one. I watched from behind those eyes as he struck the friend to the ground and then lifted him up off of his feet and slammed him into the wall. I watched from behind those eyes as his friend went from shocked to terrified in a few seconds. I watched as people tried to drag us away and slowly my grasp loosened Nothing was ever quite the same after that. His friend also became distant after this as well.

Another night. His game. He was scared. He knew I was there. It had been a few months since the incident in school. Something inside him knew I was here, and this is why he wanted to attempt this game. It was some pathetic attempt to destroy me. I watched as he began to walk from one chalk x to the other. Our connection became stronger with every step. I was hovering just behind him, and he knew it. My hands stroked at the beads of cold sweat on his neck. His pace had quickened to the point of almost jogging. I could feel that he did not want to turn and look at me. However, something was changing. I could now put my hand right through his physical form. We were becoming one.

The second x was only feet away as he turned to look into my cold expressionless eyes. We were one. He was now a cloak. A mask. A lie. I could wear his like a disguise and he was completely mine to shape and mould any way I wished.

…

Now, reader, you have been strung along on this journey of half-truth. I will give you the truth of this story that he does not wish to divulge:

Sunday. Almost midnight.

Trickling blood drained down the gutter between two nightclubs. The street was quiet. Deserted. I watched from behind those eyes as three men staggered into the night. They looked like a father and his two sons. They unknowingly passed by him, lying beside a parked car. As they disappeared around a corner, he attempted to steady himself against the car but failed miserably. He slipped and smashed his face against the pavement for a second time.

I had watched earlier as he entered the pub across the street and was quickly ejected by some surly looking bouncer. It looked like it was some family gathering. The aftermath of a funeral possibly. Each member of the party had that quiet distressed look of not knowing what to say or do. The night seemed to go well. He did not even get to talk to them.

He regained consciousness for a second time. An ambulance sped past on the road beside him. He began to panic and started to hurry down the alleyway in the same direction the father and sons went.

*

About one hour has passed.

He had regained some sense of himself and moved with slightly more purpose now.

He made several detours on the simple path home. What should have only been a thirty-minute walk took around an hour. He cut through a reservoir and stopped outside an abandoned school building. He hesitated by the gates of the local hospital, tears in his eyes, before continuing on. Eventually he reached his home.

The light was on. He went inside. The house was eerily quiet. Nobody was home. The television was playing some old black and white movie. The living room was empty. The kitchen was empty. The upstairs bedrooms were empty. He entered his bedroom and slowly pulled a chair to face the doorway. He slumped down on the chair and stared out into the hall.

He sat in numbing silence as the minutes slipped into hours and the dawn slipped through the window. He had not slept all night. He had been drinking energy juice like water and concentrating on the hallway with ferocious intensity.

He stood up and shook the nights thoughts free from his head, and then headed downstairs and out the front door.

*

He arrived at college early. Foolishly early. It is just him and the cleaners. He sat by some classroom door and put his head in his hands, shutting out the world around him.

People passed by him. Students. Tutors. They ignored him. Th classroom tutor appeared and quickly glanced at him. He opened the classroom door and shut it sharply behind him. The rest of the class arrived. They ignored him.

The tutor opened the door and one by one they entered. He was the last to enter. He hesitated for the briefest of moments before heading in. Choosing a seat at the far corner he returned to staring at the floor. Some girl sat at a desk beside him. He does not show any form of recognition.

The class ended. He left quickly, dropping a sealed envelope on the tutor's desk as he passed. The tutor tried to say something, but he was now long gone. The letter was his fiction about dropping out of college for a job which he did not have.

*

Back home. He poured a glass of water and stared intently at it for a long time. There was nobody else here. He imagined fantastical scenarios in his head as the glass broke in his hands and blood began to trickle from his wrists. He screamed. People arrived. He told them it was an accident, and he was fine. He was checked over by paramedics who could not see the truth. They then left. He was left alone on the front steps.

His brother arrived. After a moment they left together.

*

They had veiled conversations with none of them touching on the real subject. His brother looked like he wanted to say something but held back for some unknown reason. He put on a good show. He wore the mask well. They then parted ways, watching as his brother disappeared into the distance. He chose to go another direction.

*

His steps were quicker and more precise this time. he had a purpose. He just didn't now it yet. Over the bridge and through the local Dam he went. He stopped abruptly as some oung couple came into view.

They were sitting on a bench. They were feeding a duck. He knew her.

I watched from behind his eyes as he was overcome with something. It is unexplainable.)ne moment he was standing quiet and alone. The next, he had dragged the boy from the bench nd was beating him bloody with his fists. The girl was screaming. Nobody could hear her. He eat her partner unconscious.

He stopped. I watched as he immediately started CPR on the unconscious partner. After few moments they jerked awake.

He stood. His eyes became fleeting and desperate. They could not focus on any one hing for very long. He muttered something to the girl and then turned and sprinted off into the ight.

*

From behind his eyes, I followed. I watched. I did not intervene. My grasp on him ently loosened and we separated. This was it. I sat down on the platform directly across from im.

He sat alone for what felt like an eternity to himself, but in reality, was only a few noments. He stood up and walked towards me. Stopping on the edge, his flickering eyes met ny own. A moment of calm fell over the station as his pupils settled on some distant horizon. He stepped forward.

I did not follow.

*

Part 3

The raven transforms.

I am in a circular room strapped to one of seven chairs. The other six chairs have reflections of me in the same predicament. All these reflections are memories of my past. A past that did not exist. Reflections I created to hide behind. Each of them appears to be just as horrified as I am.

In the centre of the circle the raven transforms into a man, cloaked in shadow. Its eyes flicker from chair to chair, eventually settling on my own. It's voice cracks at the edges as it attempts to speak.

"It's over now. You are lost inside yourself. None of them will ever question why you did what you did. None of them will remember you. They will only focus on the tragic story of losing you. They will tell stories of who they thought you were while never truly knowing the truth. You have been pondering a question for too long now. Are you good, or are you evil? The lines between good and evil are blurred with the regrets of time. I am that face in your reflection and the darkness behind your eyes. We have always been one person. I am the nightmare born inside you and I have never left your side. Slowly you let me in. I have lain dormant inside of you for years. I was there at your first cruel act, and I was there at your final breath. In those lowest moments of your life, I was the voice you turned to. I was the only part of you that you thought could survive. You never realised I was the darkest part of you and every single time you let me in I poisoned your very being. You can call me whatever you like but I am you. I was born from you and grew inside of you. I am the shadow in the dark. I am the monster behind the mask. I am the reflection you cannot bear to look at. I am you. Now it is time to face yourself once and for all."

The figure pounces on each reflection strapped to the other chairs and sinks its jaws into their necks. One by one they stop struggling. I am the only one left as it turns and faces me, dripping crimson blood in the darkness.

"I leave you now to fester and rot here forever."

I stop struggling against the restraints and stare into the creatures' eyes. Memories flood my senses as I pull them from my heart. A young child giggles with his friends as he plays in the summer sunlight. The same child hurries home from school to spend time with his brother. They laugh and joke while playing games. Old memories of friends and family rapidly flash between the two figures in the darkness. These images slow to a single image of a younger me walking alone in the rain. There is someone behind me. Watching. It is my brother. It is my father. It is my mother. It is my friends. The face changes and fades from everyone I hold close in my life. The face continues to change into that of strangers. Each one has on the same mask. The creature begins to howl in agony.

"You can leave me here, but I am not alone. I see clearly now. I have never been alone. There are people all around me who care. Family. Friends. Strangers. We are on the same path. I am willing to fight. You can knock me down again, and again, but I will always be able to pull myself back up. I am no longer afraid of you. I am no longer afraid of the truth. That is enough. I am enough."

The figure screeches in pain and transforms back into a raven, disappearing into the darkness. I am left alone with only memories and corpses of my past.

*

I am left alone at a train station, well past midnight, and drenched in sweat and regret as a train speeds past. For a moment I thought I saw something on the other side of the platform. It looked a bit like the shadow of some large bird taking flight.

It is both late and early. I am both tired and awake. It is the end of a very long day. My legs carry me back towards the bright chaotic noise and the light behind me.

*

A very-young boy stands alone in some secluded corner of a primary school. The other students are playing in the background, but this boy does not pay them any attention. He watches in fascination at what is happening in front of him.

The structure of the building means that there is a section of playground just between two buildings that can be the perfect wind-trap. One moment this little square is quiet and dormant with litter, and the next it is a whirlwind of crisp and chocolate-bar packets. Caught in the chaos of a passing breeze they create a small tornado of litter.

The young boy knows this location all too well. One foot after the other he walks, until he is directly in the centre of the chaos. The wind chills and excites him. It is in this chaos he feels the calmest.

None of the other children know he is there. None of the other children realise he is gone.

Now reader, I look directly at you. This is somewhat of an ending. Not the ending you were expecting, I suppose. I hope you found something in these pages. I do not expect everything to make sense. This story is based on one truth, and I hope it may be used to help others understand some aspect of the mindset.

There is a reason the young man in the story does not have a name and this was because it could be any young man in any town or city in the world. It could be someone reading these words. It could be someone you pass every day. It could be a family member. It could be a friend. It could be you. It was me.

This story attempts to condense some elements of my depression and attempted suicides to highlight a message. The true story is much longer and spanned over several years. I did not realise what was happening and don't think I would have been able to stop it if I did. The truth is I was locked inside my own head, and this was the wrong place to be. This internal depression and voice inside my head brought me to consider and attempt suicide on several occasions. This is where I expect to lose the people who do not understand what depression is.

Depression is real. It is not a choice. I did not choose it. Nobody does. I am not a therapist and I do not know the science behind what causes depression. All I know is how I felt. How it felt to me. How I acted. All I know is the toll it took on me for several years to the point where I almost stepped out in front of a train.

Now. I do not apologise that this is somewhat of a dark story. I obviously did not do it. I am still here, talking to you. I would like to say I have the answer to what brought me back from the darkness. I can't. I have some ideas, but they are all personal to me and I would not want to assume every victim of depression has the same elements in their lives. All I know is talking to someone helped. I took it one step at a time and eventually it weakened its hold on me.

There a million reasons to choose life. You have yours. I have mine. The ones closest in your life care deeply about you and will always be there when you need them most. If you cannot speak to them then it may help to talk to someone you do not know. There are anonymous groups who meet in person and online throughout the country. There are like-minded individuals all over the world who will understand elements of what you are going hrough. We are here. We are willing to help. Your voice is important and there will always be omeone willing to listen.

To those of you who do not understand this, I promise that you will have passed omeone suffering from depression and not realised it. We have become adept at pretending we are fine. We hide behind characters we created to avoid conversations about it. Some of us don't even realise what is happening until we are lost in it. You have the power to help. You have to power to check on friends, family, co-workers. Even strangers you pass on the street. You have the power to show someone you can see them, and you can hear their voices. This can be enough. This can be the difference between life and death.

There are hundreds of organisations out there who were created for purposes such as this. The main one being the Samaritans. However, there are local ones too. Just by having a conversation with people they are saving thousands of lives.

There are still moments today when I look into the mirror and the darkness behind my eye's stares back at me. I have a routine where every morning before I brush my teeth, I look at my reflection for about thirty seconds. I stare into my reflection's eyes, and I try to stare past what is obvious. I try to see something inside that darkness. Because it is still there. It has taken me time, and numerous conversations, to be able to overcome it. It will never truly disappear, and it is a part of who I am. Now that I know I am able to deal with it, I have some level of power over it.

Every journey begins with that first step in the right direction. The more we show we are willing to talk about depression and suicide the more likely those who need help will have a greater chance of receiving it.

I hope that makes sense.

*

Printed in Great Britain
by Amazon

21775740R00037